Slices of Life

A Storyteller Series book

Short Stories of Humor and Pathos

By Mark Wilkins

TABLE OF CONTENTS

Preface

Humor has always been an important part of my life. Humor makes the good times better and the hard times bearable. That is why I wrote this book. It is filled with humorous stories. Some are real and some fiction but all are humorous.

It is my hope that the humor in this volume will help make your good times better and your hard times bearable. Perhaps, you will find something within these pages that stays with you and you can share with others. Humor, after all, is meant to be shared.

Mark Wilkins

Author

A Matter of Perspective

Three old men were sitting on a bus bench. To pass the time they had a conversation comparing how hard their childhoods were. While the first two old men were talking, the third just sat listening.

The first old man said "When I a kid, I had to walk three miles to school every morning."

The second old man said "I had to walk four miles."

The first old man said "There were no traffic signals, I risked my life crossing the street."

The second old man said: "You had streets? I had dirt roads. I risked my life with every step I took because a car could run me over at any time."

The first old man, who was by now upset said: "I had to walk in sub-zero, freezing temperatures!"

The second old man said "I did too and our weather was so cold, my jacket froze!"

The first old man, figuring out how the second old man bested him, chimed in: "You had Jackets!"

The second old man replied: "Yes we had jackets but we were so poor my jacket was made out of paper bags."

The first old man, in an obviously lame attempt to best the second one, shouted: "Yeah? Well, when I was a kid I walked to school in temperatures so cold my shoes froze!"

To which the second old man replied: "You had shoes?"

The Third old man, who had been sitting quietly during the entire conversation suddenly spoke; "You had feet?"

Then he opened his jacket and revealed two legs cut off at the knee caps.

Sometimes we look at life from the perspectives of our own problems and in so doing, ignore how fortunate we really are.

A Smart Spouse

Bryan and Annie had been married about four years. Bryan was fifteen years older than 27 year old Annie. Annie and Bryan had a big dog. Annie had the habit of allowing the dog to climb up on her lap, touch his nose to hers and give her a big lick on her face. Bryan never really minded it. It was just one of those peculiar things a spouse does that the other spouse put up with and learns to ignore.

Annie's mother was visiting for a week. She worked very hard making a turkey dinner. The three of them sat down at the table and began eating. Suddenly, their dog Sparky put his front paws on Annie's lap and hoisted himself up. She turned her face towards him and he touched his nose to hers. Then he give her face a great big lick. The dog lowered himself down and laid down besides Annie.

Annie's mother was horrified by what she had just witnessed.

"What a pig!" she yelled. "What a pig you are Annie!"

Then she looked at Bryan. "What do you think boychic? Which of them is a pig, your dog or my daughter?"

Bryan thought for a moment before he responded.

"If you're asking me which one is a pig, my wife or my dog, the pig is always my dog." He said.

Annie chuckled with glee. "What a wonderful husband I have!"

Annie's mother quipped "But Annie is intelligent she has a brain and should know better. The dog is just a dumb dog?"

"Because tonight, when I go to sleep," Bryan replied, "I want to sleep in my bed with my beautiful, loving wife instead of in the doghouse with Sparky."

An example of "An Arrogant American"

An American woman was visiting a South American Nation. She was at a black tie dinner and saw a distinguished gentleman in a black tux passing by her.

"Hey you!" she yelled as he passed.

He stopped and addressed her. "Yes Madam."

"Could you bring me some jalapenos?" She Inquired.

"Madam," He said politely, "I am the President of this country."

"Aren't you a servant of the people?" She replied.

"No Madam, I am in charge of the people, there is a difference." He said, somewhat annoyed.

"What's the difference?" She asked as he was turning to walk away from her.

He spun around and replied "A servant of the people gets people's jalapenos for them; someone in charge of the people tells them to get their own damn jalapenos!"

How He Lost His Facebook Friends

One night, Joe was on Facebook with a bunch of friends he had known for many years. Many of them moved out of town and he hadn't actually seen them for quite a while but Facebook offered him an opportunity to keep in touch with them. On this night, they were all posting odd photos. And as one guy would post a photo, another would make a funny comment about it.

Then he saw it. A photo of an overweight, elderly looking woman staring intently at a cell phone which she held around where her belly was. Then he thought of it. A caption that would make his friends all laugh. It was cruel and biting but it fit the photo perfectly. He began typing it in the comment section and hit enter.

"Hattie hadn't seen her toes in six years, so she took a photo of them to be sure they were still there."

Within seconds his friends began to post comments back.

"You cruel bastard!" Wrote one friend.

"How dare you!" Wrote another.

"You've crossed the line, crap for brains!" Wrote a third.

And just as soon as his friends wrote those comments, they unfriended him. Joe couldn't figure out why his friends were so mad at him. Then he went back and took a good look at the photo. It was his friend's wife who had passed away the night before. He wanted to apologize but it was too late. He had no more friends left so there was no one to apologize to.

Johnny's First Hike

Johnny was a rather precocious seven year old. He had always wanted to go hiking but there was a problem. He lived in the middle of a big city and had no access to transportation. There were no forests or sprawling parks nearby. Johnny had given up hope.

Norman, his big brother said he would take Johnny. Norman was stationed at a military base 300 miles away from the city where Johnny lived. One weekend he came by and told Johnny he would take him hiking.

Norman didn't have a very good track record with Johnny. Before Johnny dreamed about hiking, he dreamed about going to the snow. Norman took him earlier in the year. Norman went skiing while Johnny was stuck in the lodge with Norman's pretty but non-assertive girlfriend Paula. He did actually see and touch the snow but that was when he was walking back to the car to go home.

Norman picked Johnny up. They sped away in Norman's brand new car. They drove for miles and miles and it looked like Norman was going to go to a forest. Then Norman got a phone call.

"We're going to have to cut our outing short." Norman said as he hung up his cell phone.

"An important meeting just came up."

Johnny was devastated. He complained that he never got to do anything. He began weeping. Johnny's weeping touched Norman's heart. He exited the freeway at the next off ramp. He drove down the street and turned down a dirt road which led to a hill. He parked his car and got out of it.

"Here we are sport." He told Johnny.

"Where is here?" Johnny responded.

"The place where we are going to go hiking," Norman replied, "We're going to hike up over that hill."

With that said, Norman and Johnny began walking up the hill. As they went further up, the dense shrubbery at the beginning of their journey began to fade away. As they reached the crest of the hill, they looked over what appeared to be a bald valley with several large mounds of dirt that looked like a giant gopher had made them. Two bulldozers parked haphazardly. There were a lot of small things strewn about the ground. Johnny couldn't make out exactly what the things were.

Norman and Johnny hiked down the hill, and began walking on the bald plain below. Johnny began to recognize the things he had seen on the ground from high above. There were some rocks and a few weeds here and there but most of what was sticking out of the ground appeared to be bits of paper, metal and plastic covered over with dirt.

As they walked further, the number of items on the ground increased. They came upon one of the giant mounds of dirt. Johnny scrambled up it. He cheered triumphantly when he got to the top. He raced back down the hill and joined Norman who was blabbing away on his cell phone, walking at ground level on the other side.

They walked a bit further and came upon one of the bull dozers. Johnny climbed up on top of hit and sat in the driver's seat. He pretended it was a tank and played tank commander for about 15 minutes while Norman just stood there continuing his cell phone conversation.

The walked another half mile. As they walked Johnny saw more and more bits of paper, plastic and metal sticking out of the ground. He played a game trying to make out what they were before they were mowed under the dirt. He saw some newspaper pages, a couple of telephone books and various cracker and cookie boxes. He saw cans of all sorts and even bottles.

Johnny suddenly stopped. He looked forward about 20 feet. He recognized something he had recently thrown out. He rushed towards it. Sure enough, it was his G.I. Joes doll. It had its left arm missing and a burn mark on its right temple. Johnny looked up at Norman.

Norman," he said. "I think we have been hiking in a sanitary landfill."

No," replied Norman, "I think we've been hiking in a garbage dump."

Kermit Ham

Kermit Ham aspired to be a star football player. Under the circumstances, however, it would take a drastic change. Kermit was in deep anguish because all he ever wanted to do was play football.

Kermit just knew that once he was accepted by a football team he would earn his spot in the starting lineup. He knew that once he began playing, he would be intent on winning the game. He was certain he would make a significant contribution to that team's victory.

Kermit's need to play football was urgent and he was devoted to becoming a football player. He spent hours imagining himself making plays and running patterns. He longed for the excitement of being part of a team and the idea of crowds of people cheering him on to victory.

His mother crushed his lifelong dream when she told him that it was impossible. She told him that he would have to be happy with sitting in his own crap eating whatever slop was put in front of him. Besides, she said, he had a lot of relatives at work on football fields across the world and none of them were happy.

Why was it impossible for Kermit to be an NFL Star? It was impossible because Kermit was a pig. The relatives he had working on football fields were not playing football, they were covering the football.

Little Arnie and the Vicious Dogs

Little Arnie was a thin, frail boy of 13. His mother left for work at 6 o'clock every morning, so Arnie had to walk the three miles to his middle school. About half way through his three mile journey he passed a house with a fenced front yard. Tow gigantic Doberman Pinchers lied in that yard.

Every day, when Arnie passed by the house, the two Doberman's would charge the part of the fence that Arnie was passing, barking and snarling all the way. As they came upon the fence they always lunged towards Arnie making horrible, scary growling noises. They snapped at the fence and tried to stick their noses through the natural holes in the chain link fencing and bite Arnie. They would hit the fence with such sped and ferocity that many times, Arnie thought it would give way, allowing the dogs to escape and bite and even eat Arnie.

Day after day, Arnie dreaded that part of his journey to and from middle school. He knew it would only be a matter of time before the two vicious dogs would actually knock over the fence and mutilate or even eat his thin, frail body. Arnie decided to do something about it.

He went to his local drug store and bought a box of Ex Lax laxative pills. As he walked to school the next day, he pulled each pill out of its wrapping and put the pills in his pocket. Then, as he passed by the house with the Dobermans, he tossed all of the pills over the fence. The dogs continued to charge and bark and snarl and snap at him but upon looking back, he noticed them starting to check out the pills after he passed by.

On his way back from school Arnie passed by the house with the vicious Dobermans. He didn't hear them barking or charging. He walked up to the fence (something he was afraid to do before), held onto it and peered into the yard. He say the two Dobermans laying listlessly near the front door of the house, a good 60 feet from the fence.

As Arnie peered into the area, he noticed one of the dogs barely lift its head, weakly murmured a yelp and put its head back down. A strange joy rushed through Arnie's veins and his cheeks turned red as a smile lit up his face .Had he succeeded in stopping the vicious mongrels that elicited fear and dread every time he walked to of from his school? Only time would tell.

The once vicious dogs remained listless for the rest of that week. After that, when ever Arnie would pass by the house, the dogs would bark, begin to charge and them stop dead in their tracks once they say it was Arnie who was passing. He didn't really know why the dogs changed their attitude toward him. He wasn't even sure if they had done so out of fear or respect. All he knew was that they had changed and his daily walks were way less stressful because of it.

Misread Cues

The leader of one of the most powerful nations in the world went on a state visit to a third world nation. He was assigned a translator from that nation to accompany him everywhere he went. The leader of that nation had a State Dinner in his honor. Over 1500 people attended. The translator spent much of his time translating between what dinner guests were asking the leader and the leader's responses, as he visited some of the many tables that were in the grand banquet hall.

After the dinner, the leader of the third world nation introduced the powerful leader from the prosperous nation, so he could, as customary, give a speech. He got up to the podium and began speaking.

"This is my first time in your wonderful nation." He said. "I have met many wonderful people here tonight." He continued. But to his dismay, there was absolutely no reaction from the audience.

"I have talked to other government officials from my nation to see how we could help your nation." He stated. But the audience just stared at him stone faced.

In a desperate move, he walked behind that nation's leader, and as he stood over him, he put one hand on each of the man's shoulders and shouted "This man is my friend!"

The crowd began shouting "Mushy Pooshy!"

Started, but ecstatic that he seemed to get a rise out of the crowd, he shouted "Our country is going to give your country a huge amount of money in aid in the next three years!" Again the crowd shouted, "Mushy Poohsy! Mushy Pooshy!"

"In fact", he continued, "It is my sincere hope that our two nations become very close in the future!"

Again, the crowd shouted "Mushy Pooshy! Mushy Pooshy!"

Feeling triumphant, he walked out of the room and as he left, he could hear the leader of the third world nation at the microphone shouting "There he goes, a great leader from a great nation!" to which the audience even more loudly than before proclaimed "Mushy Pooshy! Mushy Pooshy! Mushy Pooshy!!!"

As he walked down the long corridor, which would exit to a waiting limousine, which would take him to the airport and a waiting plane, he repeatedly asked his translator how he thought the speech went. The translator merely replied, "It is not my place to tell you sir." Then, after walking a while, the translator abruptly stopped in front of a washroom.

He turned to the leader and said "May I ask you a favor?"

"Sure", Replied the leader.

"I am supposed to accompany you to the limousine but I ate a rather large lunch today and have to go the bathroom to make a gigantic Mushy Pooshy. May I go?"

"Of course." Came the reply as the powerful leader of the prosperous nation walked away feeling a little less triumphant.

Mama's Cell Phone

Two sisters, Sally and Jessica had an elderly mother who was always out in the streets walking around the neighborhood "visiting" with friends. Sally was worried about their mother, so she bought her a cell phone, so she could call Sally or Jessica if she needed help or in event of an emergency.

After about two weeks, the mother complained to Jessica.

" Your sister keeps on bothering me." She exclaimed. "She calls me up every few hours, asking who I've called, checking to see if I'm running up the cell phone bill. I can't take it anymore, she's driving me crazy!"

Jessica listened patiently, then responded. "What do you want me to do about it?" She said.

"I want you to get me a cell phone. Her mother replied. " Then perhaps Sally will stop bothering me about this all the time."

At the end of the month an angry Sally cancelled her mother's cell phone contract. Early the next morning, Jessica took her mother to the cell phone store and bought her a brand new cell phone. Jessica put the plan in her own name. She gave her mother a plan with 1500 minutes per month and explained to her mother that she should use the phone only when she really needed it because the company would charge 50 cents per minute for each and every minute over the allotted 1500 per month. Finally she told her mother that the phone had a freshly charged battery good for five hours of calling, so the mother didn't have to worry about running out of battery if she needed to make a call. Jessica's mother, with tears in her eyes thanked her as she hugged her.

Later that day, Jessica's mother appeared at her door. "Jessica," she exclaimed, "The phone doesn't work!"

Jessica looked over the phone. It was dead as a doornail. She immediately got into the car and took her mother back to the cell phone store and got there just before they closed. She went up to a clerk and asked him about the dead phone. He took the phone to the back of the store and appeared a few minutes later with an explanation.

"The batteries dead." He said.

"But when you guys sold this phone to me, you told me that the battery was good for five hours of calling, why is it dead?" Jessica demanded.

"It must've been used up." Came the clerk's cocky reply.

Jessica looked at her mother, "Who did you call?" She asked.

"Well," Jessica's mother replied, "My sister in Miami, Your cousin Joel in France, my Aunt Runi with the one good eye, my old boyfriend who I haven't talked to since I was 23, and a few friends from the old neighborhood."

Muscle Man

A husband and wife had been married for many years. The husband had long since passed his prime and rarely exercised. He still liked to think of himself as a handsome, well-built man. One day, his wife touched his belly, which had expanded several inches over the years, and said "Flabby".

The man took this statement to heart and resolved to do some-thing about it. He detested exercise. The next time he saw her hand move towards him he tensed his muscles. She didn't say he was flabby. Over time, the man developed the habit of tensing up whenever his wife's hand moved towards his body.

One day the wife decided to test her husband. She moved her hand towards his shoulder, he tensed up. It was rock hard. She moved her hand towards his arm. He tensed up there too, she giggled. She moved her hand to the small of his back, he tensed up there too. She giggled again. Her hand gently roamed toward the back of his thigh. He tensed up there too. She laughed.

Then, with a twinkle in his eye, he said "How do you like your muscle man?"

"I wish the man I was feeling was the man I was married to." She replied with a smirk.

Resurrecting the Jock

Carl Granite used to be a chiseled, well oiled, four sport jock when he attended John Tyler High School back in the day. All the girls longed to be his girlfriend. All the boys wished they could be him. He was popular and supremely athletic.

Now, a mere seven years later and seventy five pounds heavier, his two best friends were in much better shape and more athletic than he was. Carl knew Ralph and Bob since elementary school. He still knew them in middle school and high school. They were fortunate enough to be on the same football team in college. The difference was Bob and Ralph stayed in shape after college while Carl just let himself go.

Every Sunday Morning, rain or shine, the three of them met for breakfast at a local diner. They discussed how their week went and what they had planned for the coming week. One particular Sunday, Bob talked about a 10 K run he had just completed that week and Ralph talked about a 10 K run he was going to go on the next week. Carl longed for the joy of athletic competition and suggested that the three of them sign up for a 10 K run.

"You're not serious are you Carl?" Bob replied.

"Of course I am, Bob," He said. "It'll be fun, just like the old days."

"But Carl," Ralph replied. "You are way out of shape!"

"I am serious and I can do this." Carl stated unequivocally.

"When would you do this?" Bob inquired.

"Let's both sign up for the 10 K Ralph is running in next Saturday!" Carl suggested.

"I don't know," Bob stated. "I'm still recovering from yesterday's race." "Besides, you don't have enough time to train Carl." Ralph said with concern.

"Train?" Carl said with impunity. "I may not be in the best of shape but I shouldn't have to train much for a paltry 10 K run. I used to run marathons, remember?"

"I remember," Stated Bob. "But that was then and (he pointed to Carl's bulging gut), this is now."

Carl's face turned red and his nostrils flared.

"I'll bet you guys that, not only will I finish the 10 K next Saturday, but I will beat the both of you!" Carl stated confidently.

"You're crazy Carl!" Ralph screamed. "You are too far out of shape to finish, let alone beat us!"

"You're serious about this Carl?" Bob inquired.

Carl nodded affirmatively.

"Okay, you're on!" Bob shouted. "What's the bet?"

"Let's keep it friendly and bet ten dollars each." Carl said.

"Make it twenty." Bob replied.

The three men shook hands and agreed. Carl and Bob called that morning and signed up for the 10K race the next Saturday. The next day, Carl got up and ran a mile. He made it in 11 minutes. He felt good. On Tuesday he ran a mile and a half but his left foot began to hurt so he stopped. He rested on Wednesday and Thursday. Friday, he thought about running but fell asleep watching TV instead.

When Saturday morning arrived Carl felt pretty good. He felt a bit guilty for not training Wednesday through Friday but was happy he did well on the days he did train. Carl put on the new running clothes he bought Sunday. They smelled a little funny since he forgot to wash them after he ran in them on Tuesday but this was a race, not a smell good contest, so Carl didn't mind.

Carl was slated to be in the same heat as Bob and Ralph. He felt confident as he lined up. He eyeballed both Bob and Ralph and, for a moment felt like a true champion. Then the starting gun went off.

Carl looked up and both Bob and Ralph were gone. He sprinted to catch up to them but ran out of steam after about 100 yards. After a half mile, half of his heat had passed him by. By the time he reached the mile mark all of his heat and half of the next two heats left him behind. When he reached the half way point, the front runners from the final heat which began a half an hour after he did, started passing him up.

For the rest of the race, Carl kept huffing and puffing and chugging along stopping to rest periodically. When he reached the two mile point, a twelve year old boy passed him by. At two and a quarter miles, a six year old girl passed him. The last 100 yards a race official pointed to the runner behind him. He told Carl that was the only runner slower than him. Carl knew he would have to beat her or come in dead last.

Carl knew was determined to beat her so he could come away from this race with t least a shred of dignity intact. He got his legs moving faster. His nostrils were flaring. His heart was pounding. He poured it on despite the pain but the 300 pound, seventy year old woman was too much for him and she beat him to the finish by three seconds.

Rose's Wild Ride

Gepetto Coconoseo was a nice man but he was kind of stupid. He would always allow his girlfriend Rose to borrow his brand new car. Rose was known throughout the County as a notoriously horrible driver. Word of her horrible driving even made its way to Washington D.C. and The President of The United States of America compared her driving to the steering of the cars in Mr. Toad's Wild Ride at Disneyland.

One day in particular, Gepetto lent her his car and she called on her friends, two Greek Women named Nazine and Nizane to orchestrate their adventures. Nazine decided that they should go shopping for a new pair of shoes for her Aunt the 68 year old, 400 pound Bazumi. Rose picked Nazine, Nizane and Bazumi up and raced down Washington Street towards the fancy new mall.

As Rose approached the mall, the roar of the Mercedes engine attracted the attention some workers crossing the street. As Rose raced towards them, some stood staring in shock and fear while others scattered and ran for their lives. Rose swerved to avoid hitting anyone and sideswiped 13 cars parked alongside the Metro Link station. A 59 year old retired police officer who was witness to the crime, called the police and gave them the license plate number of Gepetto's brand new, now severely dented, car.

When Rose reached the mall, she parked the car. Then she, Nazine, Nizane and Bazumi left to go shop for the shoes. They had a wonderful time. They found some shoes immediately so they spent many hours shopping at other stores and having a leisurely lunch at a fancy restaurant. They emerged four hours later with a boxes of shoes and other clothing only to see the car being towed away.

"Well, said Rose with a sigh. "I guess we'll have to take the Metro Link home!"

The Pet Lamb

Josh and Bart Lamb lived in the wilds of Montana. The boys lived with their Aunt Martha. Martha was elderly and a bit senile. There was one thing she could still do well. She could cook. The boys and Aunt Martha were supported by her late husband's social security checks.

Josh, the oldest Lamb brother, was 17. He was tall, slender and adventurous. He was a boy scout and often went off on camping excursions with his scout troop. Josh was also good with animals. He had several pets including three dogs, a cat and a baby lamb.

Bart was Josh's direct opposite. He was a short fat 12 year old. His idea of adventure was watching an action movie on T.V. He liked Josh's pets but rarely played with them. He loved to eat and was spoiled by his aunt Martha's good cooking.

One day, Josh told Bart that he was going on a special outing with his scout troop. He would be gone for three weeks. He asked Bart to take care of his pets as Aunt Martha might forget to feed them or to walk the dogs. Bart agreed.

The three weeks Josh was gone were fun filled. He hiked and fished and climbed a 2,000 foot peak. The other scouts told him ghost stories by the fire at night and together they stalked wild animals with cameras. He thought about Bart, Aunt Martha, his dogs, cat and lamb constantly and hoped that all was well with them. At the conclusion of the three weeks, Josh's scoutmaster drove all the boys in his troop home in his minivan.

When the minivan came to Josh's property, Bart was waiting by the side of the road. Josh asked Bart if everything was okay. Bart said that things were pretty good. Josh asked about Aunt Martha. Bart said she was okay. Josh asked about his three dogs. Bart said they were good. Josh asked about his pet cat. Bart said that she was good. Josh asked about his pet lamb. Bart didn't reply. Josh asked again. Bart still didn't reply.

Finally Josh asked Bart "How about my pet lamb, was she good?

"Good," Bart replied. "She was delicious!"

The Communal Lunch

A group of seven men worked at a small factory. They did not get paid very much and there were no decent restaurants in the immediate area so they all brought food from home for lunch. The food they brought needed to be warmed up. They all had lunch at the same time and the lunchroom had no microwave only a stove. The stove's broiler did not work. Its oven did not work. It didn't have burners on the top like most stoves, the entire surface of the top of the stove was a grill.

For a while the men would rotate to take turns using the stove but that only allowed a maximum of four or five of them to heat up their lunch food. Every day, two or three of the men would be unhappy because they had to eat a cold lunch. This went on for a few weeks until one day, when three of the men, Pablo, Juan and Miguel took their lunches, threw them on the grill of the stove. Miguel brought skirt steak, Juan brought chunks of potato and Pablo brought sliced green peppers, red peppers and onions. The three men cooked their food together and had fajitas. Once the other men saw this, they wanted to do the same thing. Then Pablo had the idea of all seven men each bringing something different and having one man cook it. The daily tradition of sharing a communal lunch was born.

The communal lunch went on for several years. Each of the seven men specialized in brining something to the meal. Miguel always brought some kind of meat because his brother worked in a butcher shop and his boss let him take home day old meat. Juan always brought some kind of potato because he lived near some potato fields and there were always potatoes that spilled onto the sidewalk next to the fields. Pablo had a vegetable garden so he always brought vegetables. Luis

always brought tortillas because his wife worked at a tortilla factory. Gabriel always brought desert because his wife worked at a bakery and she got to take home day old pastries. Marcos always brought liquid refreshment because his brother drove a soft drink truck.

The seventh man however, Jose, always brought Spanish rice sandwiches. Spanish rice sandwiches consisted of cold Spanish rice between two slices of white bread. They were always cold, always flavorless and he always brought three. No one ever ate any of Jose's sandwiches. He never ate any of his sandwiches. He always ate the food the other men prepared. He had even been seen taking home the leftovers, whenever there were any.

One day, when Jose was absent from work, the other men began to talk about how Jose had always managed to eat everyone else's food without making a meaningful contribution himself. The group had decided to kick Jose out of the communal lunch and sentence him to a lifetime of eating his cold Spanish rice sandwiches. They elected Pablo to tell Juan the bad news the next day.

The next day before work began, six of the seven men gathered in the parking lot waiting for Jose to arrive. After a few minutes, Jose came walking up holding a plastic bag which the other men knew contained his three Spanish rice sandwiches. With the other men looking on, Pablo approached Jose with the thought of telling him that he and the others were sick of Jose's freeloading and that he was exiled from the communal lunch. As Jose approached however, he took a good look at him. He noticed that his clothes were quite shabby. His shirt was missing two buttons and its collar was frayed. His pants were the same that he was wearing the day before and come to think of it, all week. He looked at Jose's feet as he drew closer and could see that they had holes in their soles.

Pablo realized that he didn't really know too much about his co-worker of six years. He decided to find out before he delivered the other men's harsh verdict.

"Good morning Jose, Pablo asked, How are you today?"

"Okay," Jose replied.

"The men and I have something we'd like to ask you about." Jose stated in a very polite manner.

"Go ahead, ask it," Jose replied.

" Everyday during the communal lunch, you bring the same Spanish rice sandwiches," Pablo began.

"And we, uh, we were just wondering why?" he finally spat out.

As Jose replied, tears began to well up in his eyes, "I have no brother's or sisters that work at a butcher or a bakery. My brothers and sisters are all dead. My wife is an invalid. I have a 12 children at home. I am the only one who brings in a paycheck," he said with a trembling voice. These Spanish rice sandwiches are all my family eats every day, every meal. They aren't much but they are all I have to offer. I really look forward to these communal meals because it's the only chance I get to eat something different. I take home leftovers because it is the only chance my family gets to eat something different" He concluded.

The expression on Pablo's face changed. He looked over and saw that the other five men had changed the way they looked at Jose as well. Pablo and the other men knew that they almost made a terrible mistake. He told Jose that on this day, they were actually going to use his Spanish Rice Sandwiches. Jose perhaps for the first time in quite a while, began to smile.

That day at lunch, Pablo asked Jose for his sandwiches. He emptied out the Spanish rice and began to cook it on the grill. He cut the bread up into triangles and made toast. Integrated with all of the other wonderful items in the communal lunch the Spanish rice wasn't bad. From that day on Jose's Spanish rice sandwiches were always integrated as a part of the communal lunch. From that day on, the six other men brought more variety to the lunch menu and brought a lot of extra food. From that day on there were always a lot of leftovers for Jose to bring home.

The Inquisitive Fool

There is a young man we know whose name is Lance. He is a good looking, upper class, white male. He has graduated college with a Bachelor of Arts degree in Liberal Studies. He has led a life of privilege. He has traveled the world but only speaks English. He is polite but because he is totally self-absorbed, he often does things that others think of as inconsiderate. He is highly inquisitive. He had lived at home all of his life with a butler and maids to take care of him. Now that he is 25 he has decided to move out and has begun living on his own. No longer in a cloistered environment, under the protection of mama and papa, he has been unleashed upon the world. He is The Inquisitive Fool.

The Brief Incident

One day Lance was strolling down the aisle of a department store. He was looking for a few pairs of underwear. He saw a pretty, young sales clerk walking by. He decided to make his move.

"Excuse me madam." Lance stated.

The young lady turned around and saw how handsome Lance was. "Yes," She replied.

"Can you help me pick out some new pairs of underwear?" Lance said.

"Boxers or briefs." The clerk replied.

"Briefs." Lance replied.

"What size are you?" She Asked.

"I'm unsure." Lance replied.

She looked down at his crotch. He was obviously happy to see her.

"I'd say you are a large," She said.

"Okay," Lance said awkwardly.

"How come you don't know what size underwear you wear?" She asked.

"Mama usually picks out my underwear." He said.

"Are you a big mama's boy?" She inquired.

"I don't know what you mean." Lance asked.

"You know, a mama's boy, someone who loves their mama." She explained.

"Oh, yes, I do love mama. Don't you love your Mama?" He asked with a puzzled look on his face.

"Of course I love my mama," She Replied. "But it's odd for a man to love his mama too much, you know, like some kind of big mama's boy." She concluded.

"I'm confused." He said. Are you saying I'm big and I'm a mama's boy or are you saying that my mama is big and I am her boy?" He continued.

"Neither." She said. "I just wanted to know if you're a mama's boy because you said your mama usually picks out your underwear for you." She enlightened him.

"Oh," He said. "Well, I do love my mama and she does pick out my clothes for me but I still don't understand if you are saying that I am big or that Mama is big because, I assure you, neither of us are."

"I'm not saying either of you are big, I use the word big to emphasize the degree to which you are a mama's boy." She stated in an angry tone.

"I don't believe I am a mama's boy at all." He said.

"Oh, we've already established that you are a mama's boy, now we are merely determining the degree of your mama's boyism." She said as she handed him a package of tighty-whitey briefs.

Just then, another customer asked the young lady for help and she went off to help that person.

Lance just stood there dumbfounded, wondering what he might have done to upset the woman so.

The Inquisitive Fool 2

The Hole Story

Lance was walking down a crowded street. He inadvertently stepped on a woman's foot. He didn't notice and kept on walking. He hadn't gotten more than a step or two away from her when the woman yelled "ASSHOLE!" at the top of her lungs.

Lance stopped and turned around. He looked at the woman, wondering if she was trying to communicate with him.

She looked him directly in the eye and shouted "ASSHOLE!"

"Are you talking to me?" Lance inquired.

She repeated "Asshole!"

Lance thought that perhaps the woman was injured. "Are you in pain madam?" Lance asked.

"No, asshole. She replied.

Lance thought for a minute. Perhaps she didn't speak English and that word meant something in her language.

He got really close to the woman. He began speaking to her very slowly and very loudly. "You in America. We Speaky De English here!" What you Speak? Speaky de English?" He shouted

The Woman's eyes bulged out. "You are the biggest asshole in the world!" She shouted at the top of her lungs.

The Woman shouted so loudly, all of the traffic on the street both auto and foot traffic stopped. Every living creature on the street turned to stare at the woman and at Lance, the target of her tirade.

Lance responded. "How could you even say that?" he replied. "Have you seen every asshole in the world?"

"What?" replied the woman incredulously.

"And how did you get everyone to pull down their pants?" Lance continued.

"And how did you measure them, if mine is, as you say, the biggest?"

Convinced that she had encountered an escapee from the insane asylum, the woman turned around and ran away from Lance as fast as her feet would carry her.

Lance Shouted after her. "That's right, that's what you get for making claims that you can't substantiate!"

The Inquisitive Fool 3

The Pedi Cure

One day Lance Looking for a salon so he could get a pedicure. His toenails had gotten out of control and he had been getting pedicures since the age of eight, so he was used to them. He used to go to Mrs. Boston's Salon, the one his mother went to. Now that he was on his own, Mrs. Boston was a bit pricey for him. He was driving down the street and saw a nail salon in a strip mall. It was named Sally's Happy Toe. He decided to give it a try.

He parked the car and walked over to the salon. He noticed a bunch of foreign writing on the window. A middle aged Asian woman greeted him as he entered.

"Hello sir, are you here to get a gift certificate for your wife?" She asked.

"No, I would like a pedicure though." He replied.

"Oh, yes!" She stated.

"How much are they?" Lance inquired.
"$22.50." She replied.

"Okay." Lance replied.

The woman led lance to a barber chair with a foot tub in front of it. Lance sat down. Another Asian woman came over and took Lances shoes and socks off. She grimaced when she saw his toes. She put his feet in the foot tub and began filling it with warm water. Lance leaned back, and closed his eyes, enjoying the sensation of the warm water cascading over his feet.

The feeling was so pleasant and Lance was so relaxed, he almost fell asleep. Then he felt something lifting one of his feet. The woman who was giving him a pedicure began working on one of his feet. As she worked she began talking in a foreign tongue. Another woman was talking to her. She was also talking in a foreign tongue. They talked for a few minutes and as they gabbed on, Lance began to become self-conscious. He just knew they were talking about his feet. Then the woman set his first foot down and picked up his other foot. The two women burst into laughter. That's it! Lance was certain that these two women were making fun of his feet. He opened his eyes suddenly.

The woman who was talking to the woman who was giving Lance the pedicure shrieked. The woman who was giving Lance the pedicure, heard the shriek and startled, dropped Lance's foot back into the tub.

"Oh, I am sorry sir." She said apologetically. "But you startled me." She continued.

"I could have sworn you were talking about me." Said Lance.

"Oh no sir," She Replied. "We would never do anything like that." She concluded.

"I don't enjoy people speaking in another language when they are around me." Lance stated.

    The two women didn't speak the rest of the time Lance was getting the pedicure. When the woman was finished Lance walked over to the cash register. The same woman who greeted Lance when he came in was there.

"$22.50" she said.

Lance gave her two twenty dollar bills.

"Would you like to leave a tip for the girl who gave you the pedicure?" She asked.

"I would certainly not." Lance replied with a tinge of anger in his voice.

"Why, was something not to your liking?" She inquired.

"I shall not be frequenting this establishment again madam!" He stated.

"Why not?" She pressed.

"Because I feel uncomfortable being in places where people speak in a foreign language right in front of me." He stated.

"Then perhaps you should move somewhere where there are no foreigners." She replied.

"Where would that be?" Lance inquired.

"A desert island." She Retorted.

The Bad Smell

Garth and his wife Beth had been living in their small, one bedroom home for a little over a year. They had seen but not gotten to know many of their neighbors. The two they had come to know were different as night and day.

One of the two was Mr. Bobbins. He was a retired heating and air conditioning installer. He had a pulse on everything that was going on in the neighborhood. Garth or Beth sought answers from Mr. Bobbins whenever they had a question about the neighborhood, its history, any of the neighbors they didn't know or anything that was happening. Mr. Bobbins was always knowledgeable and friendly.

Boris Simmons was the other neighbor Garth and Beth had come to know. An unemployed, perennial drunk, he never knew much about anything. Garth and Beth said hello to him on occasion to which he replied with a grumble or a slathering of curse words. Boris was not a happy man. He had no job but he had cars. He had cars in his garage, cars in his backyard, cars in his driveway, cars on his front lawn and cars parked on the street. All of his cars were either barely running or not running at all. All of Boris' cars were classics of one kind or another. He fixed them up and sold them off but he hadn't sold more than a couple since Garth and Beth moved in.

One Saturday, Garth smelled a really bad odor. It first hit his nose about 7:00 a.m. when he walked down his driveway to get the morning newspaper. As the day progressed, the smell got steadily worse until 5:30 p.m. when Garth couldn't take it anymore. He walked across the street to Mr. Bobbin's house and knocked on his door.

Mr. Bobbins answered the door. Garth told him about the smell and asked where it could be coming from. Mr. Bobbins told Garth that a few of the houses in the neighborhood were still on septic tanks, perhaps it was one of them. Then, he suggested that it could be a dead animal. Mr. Bobbins agreed to sniff around and try and find out where the bad odor was coming from. Garth went back into his house and waited for Mr. Bobbins to come by with the answer.

A half an hour later, Mr. Bobbins knocked on Garth's door. He told Garth he found where the odor was coming from. Garth and Beth followed Mr. Bobbins down the street. He stopped at their neighbor's house.

"It's coming from this house." He said confidently as he pointed to Boris Simmons house.

"Boris?" replied Beth in obvious disbelief. "Are you sure?" she continued.

"This nose never lies." said Mr. Bobbins pointing to his nose.

"What does it smell like to you Mr. Bobbins?" Garth asked.

"Smells like a backed up septic tank!" Bobbins replied. "Only thing is," he continued

"Boris is not on septic; he hooked up to the sewer five years ago."

"Perhaps it's a dead animal," Beth said, hoping that is wasn't.

"No dear," Garth said. "That's not a dead animal smell." He continued.

"What does it smell like to you Garth?" Mr. Bobbins inquired.

Garth took a moment and sniffed the air, then pronounced, "Earlier, I would've sworn it was raw sewage," he stated. "But now, it smells like a natural gas leak." He concluded.

"There aren't any natural gas vents around here." Mr. Bobbins stated emphatically.

"Maybe it's in Boris' house." Garth guessed. "I'll just go knock on his door." He said as he took a few steps towards Boris' door.

"Wait honey!" Beth shouted. "There are no lights on in his house, if there is a gas leak and he's in there, he may turn one on when you knock causing the gas to explode!" She cautioned.

Thinking about what Beth said, Garth stopped dead in his tracks, took out his cell phone and called 911. He reported a possible natural gas leak and gave Boris' address. The 911 operator dispatched a fire truck. Just then, Boris Simmons emerged from his backyard with a can of beer in his hand.

"What's this about an explosion?" He said quixotically.

"Boris!" shouted Beth, "Something stinks on your property!"

Boris thought a second and then lifted the beer free arm and sniffed his armpits.

"No Boris," Garth said. It smells like a gas leak."

"I don't think there's any gas left on in my house." Boris stated.

Just then a fire truck rolled up. A platoon of fire men emerged. They talked to Garth who told them he thought there was a gas leak. The firemen agreed that they thought it didn't smell like gas but it did smell like sewage or perhaps toxic. They walked around Boris' house. They shined a powerful flashlight in the open crawl

space under his house, looking for a dead animal but found nothing but spiders. They got Boris permission and cautiously entered his house but found no gas leaks. Then they followed Boris into his back yard. Fifteen minutes later they emerged. The lead fireman walked up to Garth.

"Are you the man who called 911?" He inquired.

"Yes I am." Garth replied.

"We found the cause of that bad smell." He said.

"Was it a gas leak?" Garth replied. "I only called 911 because I thought the neighborhood might blow up." He continued.

"It wasn't a gas leak." The fireman replied. "It was an over charged car battery."

Garth thought for a moment. He felt stupid. He called 911 out of a safety concerned and all it turned out to be was a lousy car battery.

"I'm so sorry I wasted your time." Garth mumbled, half ashamed.

"You didn't waste our time." The fireman stated. "That odor was given off by sulfur in the battery venting, from being overcooked. It wouldn't have exploded, might never have caught on fire but it was somewhat toxic, especially to the small animals and pets that live in the area. You might have saved the life of a squirrel or someone's cat." He concluded.

With that the firemen loaded onto the fire truck. It turned around and roared off into the sunset. Boris went back into his backyard, somewhat embarrassed, Mr. Bobbins went home and Garth walked Beth back to their house felling a little less foolish. As he turned his key into the lock on their front door Beth began to speak.

"Honey," she said, "I think I'll call 911 about the toxic waste in our house." She said with a tinge of anger in her voice.

Garth turned around, somewhat shocked and replied "What toxic waste?"

Beth smiled and replied "You left a pair of dirty underwear on the floor of our bedroom this morning."

The Power of Soda

Two classmates were unlikely friends. Virginia was a very devout catholic. Pam was disillusioned catholic with an addictive personality. One day after school, Pam asked Virginia to join her for a soda.

"No thank you", replied Virginia, "I gave up soda for lent."

"That's funny," Pam responded, "I gave up lent for soda."

The Curse of the Angry Gypsy Woman

Big Joe Mc Gillicuddy was a giant of a man. At almost seven feet tall and 403 labs he lumbered along and, if he was in the right place, the earth would tremble as he walked. He was a gentle giant who would never intentionally harm anyone. He was also very clumsy and often banged into things, knocked over things, bumped into people or stepped on their toes. He never had any problems because even the meanest person would pause lashing out in anger once they saw Big Joe.

One day, Big Joe was in the Supermarket looking at oranges when he accidentally stepped on a woman's big toe. The woman, a gypsy, cursed him.

She said, "I curse you for stepping on my beloved big toe!"

Joe just said "sorry" in a sheepish way.

The woman didn't miss a beat and continued her curse.

"I estimate that you will get a brutal case of botulism, and diarrhea epidemic!" she continued.

Big Joe just walked away laughing to himself.\
"I don't believe in curses, they are a bunch of Hooey!" he muttered under his breath.

Big Joe walking away made the Gypsy Woman even more angry at him and she yelled loudly across the aisles towards him.

"And while you are contagious you will expose your courageous family to athlete's foot fungus!"

Joe just walked away faster slightly embarrassed but still, delighted by the woman making a fool of herself.

"But first, your nose will fall off!"

Hearing this, Big Joe began laughing hysterically as he walked further away.   Then his nose fell off.

The Futility of Holding Grudges

When I was a dean of students at a high school in the inner city of a major metropolitan school district I learned a lot lessons about holding grudges. The school is located in a one mile area where there have been as many 26 homicides in a six month period. I am in charge of discipline. There are many local gangs in the neighborhood and some of their members are among our students. We average about three fights per week. About half are fights between two boys, the other half are between two girls. Most of the fights are for stupid, childish reasons. Many are for perceived disrespect. Most of the perceived disrespect that pits one child against another is not for something the people fighting said or did to each other but for something a friend told them the other person said or did. In other words, a majority of the fights are over rumor or innuendo, not actual, personal experience.

Much of the time, when I bring the pettiness of the reasons for the anger between the two parties to their attention, both parties realize their stupidity and cool their mutual anger. If that doesn't work I bring to their attention the fact that they have been manipulated like puppets by their friends and acquaintances. That usually brings them to their senses. The icing on the cake however, is when I let them know the consequences for their fighting. Consequences can range from a one day suspension from school or in the case of bodily injury, a citation. The results of a citation are both students involved in the fight have to appear before a judge with their parents and pay a $450 fine. They could also end up with a criminal record. Severely violent students are not issued a citation; they are merely taken to Juvenile Hall / Jail. Just going over the range of consequences often gets student s to cool their tempers.

The worst cases are those where the anger between the two parties results in a grudge for life. In my experience this happens most often between girls. Some of the fights result from deep seated anger over something that happened as many as seven or eight years before. It is very difficult to stop someone with a grudge because consequences, no matter how callus, don't mean as much to them as satisfying their need for revenge.

A grudge did infect a good friend of mine. He was about 40 at the time. He was dating a woman who he desired a lot. Another friend of his, let's call him Michael, was friends with the girl and when she confided that my friend was mistreating her, Michael told her to not to accept that kind of disrespect. As a result she dumped my friend. My friend was devastated and very angry. He was not only mad at the woman but at Michael as well.

I don't know what other things he may have done to them but I do know that he voiced his displeasure with them on answering machine for his home phone. My friend often created his own messages on his answering machine. He would play a song he liked in the background and give "Shout Outs" (sing the praises of the virtues of his friends) over the music. After this event however, he changed his tune. He played a song he liked but instead of giving shout outs to his friends he went into a 3 minute diatribe about what a crappy person Michael was. He didn't even use Michael's correct last name (he probably couldn't pronounce it). Instead, he called him Michael Mahatey. After that, it was very difficult to get in touch with my friend. He didn't return phone calls. I would call him periodically and the message with the diatribe stayed on his machine for over a year. Undaunted, I would leave him messages asking my friend how he was doing or about us getting together but he never responded.

That Christmas, I got a Christmas card from him. It was a very beautiful and had the words "Happy holidays and best wishes for the new year" printed on it. Inside, he wrote a personal message. "I hope you are doing well, I'm good and want to wish you the merriest Christmas ever." Followed by the words "I don't deal with that asshole Michael anymore, he turned a female I was dealing with against me so now his ass is cut off." I immediately tried to call my friend but I got his answering machine. To my surprise, he had recorded a lovely Christmas carol. He added a nice voice over. I thought perhaps he was finally out of his grudge as I listened to his voice in a deliberate, soft spoken style utter the words…"Christmas, a season of joy and love and forgiveness. I want to wish all of you a joyful Christmas and a happy new year… and then his voice changed to a more harsh tone as he said "Except for you Michael Mahatey, you can rot in hell! " Then his voice changed to a softer tone as he uttered "Be so kind as to leave a message."

My friend had allowed his anger to permeate his every waking thought. I am certain that he was more tortured by it than he would have been if he just let it go and moved on. I am sure he is a changed man and will remain so until either time or compassion convince him to let his anger go. That is the ultimate futility of grudges; they consume you leaving little time for the things you could be accomplishing in your life.

The International Misunderstanding

Kay Kay was a woman in her mid forties. She had never left the United States. She decided to go to sunny Mexico. Even though she didn't speak the language, she thought it would be a fun, new experience to go somewhere where nobody knew her. She packed her suitcase and boarded the plane from Minneapolis to Puerta Villarta with no problem at all.

When Kay was on the plane, the stewardess came by and distributed customs forms. Luckily they had English translations written below the Spanish text. Kay got out her passport, filled out the forms and then took a nap. She totally forgot that she had put her passport and the form in the back magazine holder pocket in the seat in front of her.

The stewardess woke Kay up 15 minutes after the plane landed. Kay noticed that the plane was almost empty. Panicked, she got her suitcase and ran off the plane. She waited in the customs line at the airport for about 45 minutes. Walked up to the burly Mexican Customs Agent and he began to speak.

"Passporte." He stated briskly.

Kay fumbled around in her purse but couldn't find her passport. Her face turned beet red. The Customs Agent picked up on her embarrassment immediately.

"Que es tu nombre?" He asked.

"Me nombre?" She said sheepishly.

"Si." He said.

"(612) 555-1212."She replied.

"No senora, no numero de telefono, tu nombre." The Customs Agent replied

"Mi number es Paco." He continued.

"Kay." Kay replied

"Tu nombre." The Customs Agent repeated.

"Kay." Kay replied.

"Tu nombre." The Customs Agent repeated a little more agitated.

"Kay." Kay replied a little louder.

"Dios Mio." The Customs Agent stated.

"Y tu apellido." He continued. "Mi apellido is Sanchez."

"Kay." Kay replied.

"Por que tu no intiendo?" The customs Agent stated. Tu nombre y tu appellido?

Kay, Kay." Stated Kay

"Que? Que?" The customs Agent stated with disbelief.

"Si," Kay replied.

"Que Si?" Questioned the Customs Agent.

"No," Kay stated, "Kay Kay!"

The Customs Agent was really fuming. "Porque, Que Que?"

"I'm not Porky!" Replied Kay angrily. "In fact I'm quite thin!"

Just then the stewardess walked up with Kay's passport and customers form in hand.

"You left this on the plane madam." The stewardess said.

Kay handed the passport and form to the Customs Agent. He took one look at the passport and a big smile came onto his face.

"Kay, Kay!" He stated with a joy and relief in his voice.

He stamped both the form and the passport and handed Kay's passport back to her.

Kay took her passport and as she walked off she said "And I'm not porky!"

Author Biography
Mark Wilkins
A Storyteller

My name is Mark Wilkins. I am best known to my readers as A Storyteller. I pen the A Storyteller Series of Books for Love Force International Publishing. Unlike most other book series, it does not concentrate on a particular character or a particular story line. Instead, it focuses on books of short stories in various genres by a particular author, namely myself. Some of the books in the A Storyteller Book Series include serious fiction (A Week's Worth of Fiction), humorous fiction (Slices of Life) and a mixture of serious and humorous fiction and non-fiction (Classroom Confessions) and supernatural Fiction (Stories of The Supernatural).

The readers who enjoy my books like reading that sparks their imagination. They like stories with memorable and quirky characters on unusual topics. They like unexpected twists and turns in the plot. If any of these things my readers enjoy describe you, then you too will enjoy my writing.

I am comfortable writing in many different genres. I write both humorous and serious fiction. Some of my stories are based on true events, others are totally my invention. It is up to you, the reader, to decide which stores are based on factual events and which are completely my invention because I'm not telling. I like to tell stories and I work very hard at making those stories both compelling and entertaining. I hope you enjoy reading my books.

Kindle Books by Love Force International Publishing

Whether you are interested in true stories, fiction, humor, action, adventure, spiritual insights, quotes, poetry, self-help or children's books, Love Force international has got you covered.

NOTE: Books with AINs are available now the others will be available soon. Books with an SP after the title also have a version translated into Spanish.

The Reader Series is a series of readers that are a sampling of writings by one or more authors.

The Prophet of Life Reader (10 Book Sampler) What do cell phone addiction, a smart spouse, faith, a gangster, your reputation, spiritual DNA and a rotten egg war have in common? They are all in this sampling of stories, poems and other writings from 10 of The Prophet of Life's Kindle books.

Author: The Prophet of Life   **ISBN:** 978-1-936462-07-0 **ASIN:** B015D716C0

The Mark Wilkins Reader 10 Book Sampler!
One story from each of the ten books by Mark Wilkins. Whether its smart spouses, inquisitive fools, teachers, gangsters or ghosts this book gives you a good sampling of stories by the man known throughout the world as A Storyteller. Within its pages you will find horror, humor and pathos.

Author: Mark Wilkins   **ISBN:** 978-1-936462-38-4
ASIN:
The Love Force International Reader 15 Book Sampler!
Whether you want true crime, humor, children's stories, a ghost story, controversy, poetry or quotes this book has got all of those and more! A sampling of 15 different books by three different authors offered in Kindle books published by Love Force International.
Edited by Evan Lovefire **ISBN: ASIN:**
The Love Force International Sampler, Spanish Edition SP
This book contains a sampling of 9 different books by three different authors translated into Spanish. The books translated include What Faith has Taught me, Controversy, True Stories of Inspiration & General interest and Quotes about God by The Prophet of Life, Stories of The Supernatural and Slices of Life and Classic Children's Stories You've Likely Never Heard by Dr. Goose.
Edited by C. Gomez **ISBN: ASIN:**

The True Stories Series is a series of books which include true stories by The Prophet of Life.

True Stories!

A riveting collection of true stories. Whether you want to know about the toddler taken by a gator at a Disney Resort, an 18 year old who doesn't exist, which popular restaurant chain has a corporate mentality of public humiliation for its employees or an alarming new trend that could affect your household this book has got it all and they are all absolutely true!

Author: The Prophet of Life   **ISBN:** 978-1-936462-16-2
ASIN:

True Stories: Inspiration and General Interest   SP

What do cell phone addicts, George Orwell, birds, Paul McCartney, The Nobel Prize, Black Friday, Led Zeppelin, garbage, a pep talk, tipping, Steve Jobs, Shakespeare, inspirational thoughts and your mother have in common? They are in true stories in this book. True Stories of Inspiration & General Interest brings together stories and poems about celebrities, trends and everyday people. Sometimes surprising, always interesting, it will entertain you and give you something to think about at the same time.

Author: The Prophet of Life   **ISBN:** 978-1-936462-15-5
ASIN: B00TXWVNUC

Controversy   SP

What do Caitlyn Jenner, Donald Trump, a cure for AIDS, Chinese hackers, Adolf Hitler and Global Warming have in common? They are all at the heart of a controversy and there are stories about them in this unique book that turns tabloid headlines inside out.

Author: The Prophet of Life   **ISBN:** 978-1-936462-19-3
ASIN: B016MWU8NS
True Stories of Crime and Punishment
This book of serious crime stories is ripped from headlines
all over the globe. From the family that vanished, to the 11
year old girl killed in a fight over a boy, to the prisoner
who hasn't eaten in 14 years, to the severed human head
found near the famous Hollywood sign these stories ripped
will astound you and give you pause to think.
Author: The Prophet of Life **ISBN:** 978-1-936462-17-9
ASIN: B01406YZBE

Strange but True!
A collection of facts and stories about people, places and
things that are strange and seem like fiction but are
absolutely true!
Author: Mark Wilkins **ISBN: ASIN:**

The A Storyteller Series is a unique book series. Instead of concentrating on a particular character or genre, the series consists of collections of short stories by Author Mark Wilkins, Also Known As A Storyteller.

Slices of Life Volume 1

SP

is a collection of humorous short stories about life. Most of them deal with marriage and family members. From smart spouses to intelligent little children to guys trying to impress their friends and in-laws trying to master technology each story is like a little slice of life but together, they make up an irresistible pie. Sit back, grab a cup of coffee and enjoy some slices of lie because, before you know it, you will have finished the whole thing.
Author: Mark Wilkins **ISBN:** 978-1-936462-11-7 **ASIN:** B014ZF5VY0

Slices of Life Volume 2

This sequel to Slices of Life has more humorous stories about the rich, the poor and the middle class. It even has a story about one of their pets. Ignorance is the main theme of this book, ignorance that has consequences that are sometimes touching but always humorous. So brew so coffee or tea, sit down and relax and enjoy another satisfying batch of more slice of life because, before you know it, you will have devoured the whole thing.
Author: Mark Wilkins **ISBN:** 978-1-936462-12-4 **ASIN:**
Stories of The Supernatural Volume 1
SP

Ghosts, demonic creatures, and Death. This collection of Short Stories will haunt and entertain you. Whether it's the classic evil of A Lump of Coal or the whimsy of A Ghost in the House this collection of Short Stories and poems will haunt, thrill and entertain you.

Author: Mark Wilkins **ISBN**: **978-1-936462-18-6**
ASIN: B01M1N1QR5

Stories of The Supernatural Volume 2
SP

In this sequel to Stories of The Supernatural there are more Ghosts, Demonic Creatures and Death. This collection of short stories Centers of Ghosts and Monsters. Within its pages you will marvel at the exploits of The Soul Collector, Shudder at the mention of the dreaded Bungadun and of the Hell Banger and ride the rails on the ghost train. Strap on your seat belts, its going to be a bumpy ride! **Author:** Mark Wilkins **ISBN: 978-1-936462-26-1 ASIN:** B01MDJMSUY

A Week's Worth of Fiction:

7 unusual stories of fiction that explores different sides of the genre. From what is going through the mind of a suicide bomber to a teacher on the edge sanity to an everyman who becomes a hero through senseless violence a journey of dark adventures awaits you.

Author: Mark Wilkins   ISBN: 978-1-936462-13-1
ASIN: B01521SQ02

A Week's Worth of Fiction Volume 2
From a girl battling a corporation over the rights to her blood to people engaging in life and death struggles this sequel to A Week's Worth of Fiction gives you 7 more stories that will thrill you, surprise you and make you think. Often dystopic and sometimes surreal, if you want stories you will never forget you only need to count to 7.

Author: Mark Wilkins   **ISBN:** 978-1-936462-14-8
ASIN: B01LX9RZH7
A Week's Worth of Fiction Volume 3
From a woman trying to find love before her looks fade to
a sky marshal struggling with racism to how Karma affects
the life of a sanitation worker, this sequel to A Week's
Worth of Fiction gives you 7 more stories that will thrill
you, surprise you and make you think. Often dystopic and
sometimes surreal, if you want stories you will never
forget you only need to count to 7.
Author: Mark Wilkins   **ISBN:**   **ASIN:**
A Week's Worth of Fiction Volume 4
From a soldier trying to solve a mystery to an indigenous
man fighting barbaric tribal customs to a study of good and
evil with a surprise outcome this sequel to A Week's
Worth of Fiction gives you 7 more stories that will thrill
you, surprise you and make you think. Often dystopic and
sometimes surreal, if you want stories you will never
forget you only need to count to 7.
Author: Mark Wilkins   **ISBN:**   **ASIN:**

Classroom Confessions Volume 1
SP
is a series of true stories from the front lines of public
education. Within its pages you will meet quirky
characters, the good, the bad and the over caffeinated.
Some of them are teachers, some students and some are
administrators. Some will make you laugh, others will
make you cry but they all play an important role in public
education. Their stories are written in way that will
entertain you and give you something to think about.
Author: Mark Wilkins **ISBN**: 978-1-936462-08-7
ASIN: B00VNFJBX8

Classroom Confessions Volume 2
 Is another series of true stories from the front lines of
public educations. Within its pages you will meet
unforgettable characters like the French Substitute, Mr.
Happyhands, Harry Winkwater, The Bushwhacker and of
course, Julian. Some will touch your heart, others will give
you something to think about but they will all entertain
you.
Author: Mark Wilkins   **ISBN:**   **ASIN:**

The Beyond Faith Series
Is a series of books that look at life from a spiritual perspective. No matter what your faith, you will find spiritual insights in these books that will enrich your life.
What Faith Has Taught Me
SP

I am just an ordinary person who has been privileged to have a life filled with miracles and revelations. There are many times when I had nothing except faith but faith was all I needed to sustain me. My faith and my God have taught me many life lessons. This book shares some of the things my faith has taught me and the spiritual insights I have gained because of my faith.

Author: The Prophet of Life **ISBN:** 978-1-936462-03-2 **ASIN:** B01527IKT8

Finding God in A Chaotic World
The world can seem so chaotic these days. Many people long for guidance. Many others want to get closer to God. How do you find God amidst the chaos and confusion? How can you discern God's messages from the multi-media blitz we are each bombarded with every day? Some people are part of an organized religion. Others are spiritual without a particular religion. Some are still searching, All of them trying to find God.

In this book, you will learn that The Lord communicates with how The Lord communicates with you. You will learn about the True Nature of God and realize just how profound God's Love and reach are. You will learn the secret of why God's will always prevails. If you are ready for revelations that may change the way you look at life in general and your life in particular, read this book.

Author: The Prophet of Life **ISBN:** 978-1-936462-01-8 **ASIN:** B00SLLZAAU

Finding God without Religion

People of faith are not exclusive to religion. There are many who are spiritual or agnostic. They don't fit into the doctrine, rituals and congregational community of religion. In this wisdom filled volume, people of faith but without an organized religion can gain insights into life, the afterlife and God without being brow beaten or guilt tripped into conversion. This volume is Book 2 of the Revelations of 2012 Beyond Faith series. Part 1 is entitled Finding God in A Chaotic World.

Author: The Prophet of Life **ISBN:** 978-1-936462-10-0 **ASIN:** B00XKPD86K

Outrageous Humor Series
Books of stories and fake news articles for those with an off-beat sense of humor.
Outrageous Stories
This book is filled with offbeat humor articles. All of them are fictitious and many of them completely outrageous. No one is safe from being made fun of be they terrorists, Presidents, Dictators, The Movie and Record Business or couch potatoes. If you are college age or older and have an offbeat, irreverent, sense of humor, this book is for you!
Author: Mark Wilkins **ISBN:** 978-1-936462-33-9 **ASIN:** B01LY3VZJR
More Outrageous Stories
This book is filled with more offbeat humor articles. All of them are fictitious and many of them completely outrageous. No one is safe from being made fun of be they terrorists, Racists, National Holidays or the medical establishment. If you are college age or older and have an offbeat, irreverent, sense of humor, this book is for you!
Author: Mark Wilkins **ISBN:** 978-1-936462-33-9 **ASIN:**
Self Help Series
This consists of books by different authors designed to help people improve their lives.
Becoming The Person You've Always Wanted to Be SP
This self-help book offers a simple, yet profound method of making positive changes in your life. It includes a link to download exclusive, helpful companion worksheets to help you become the person you have always wanted to be.
Author: Mark Wilkins **ISBN:** 978-1-936462-39-1 **ASIN:**
Life Success Kit

Spiritual Thought Leader The Prophet of Life helps you
clarify what success really means to you through a series
of inspirational life lessons designed to give you new
perspectives on achieving success and a blueprint for
making changes in the things that are preventing you from
becoming a success.
Author: The Prophet of Life   **ISBN: ASIN:**

The Your Life in Rhyme Poetry Series

Is a series of Poetry books unlike any you have ever read whether it is an exploration of life itself through a thematic chapter on each of the various stages of life as in Reflections in The Mirror of Life, The mixture of thought provoking essays and inspirational poetry of Black in America or the exploration of a single topic as in Romance Returns or Life in Verse. The books in this series will have you rediscovering poetry in a way that will make you wonder why you ever avoided it in the first place.

Reflections in the Mirror of Life This unique book explores life through its harsh realities, pleasant diversions and positive possibilities. The book looks at modern society, the problems it faces, and the people who are a part of it. In a unique twist that's different from most books of poetry, Reflections is divided into five chapters, each of which explores a different theme woven into the fabric of modern life. The tone for each chapter is set by a free verse poem which is followed by a series of rhyming poems on that theme.

Author: The Prophet of Life **ISBN:** 978-1-936462-04-9 **ASIN:** B00V2TSAXC

Black in America is an exploration of racism through essays and poems. It spans from the beginnings of the Civil Rights movement through today. It includes a powerful new poem "Baltimore" and a perspective on the church shooting in South Carolina. It looks at people who have been lightning rods for race relations in America and has some surprising insights into the people and events that have shaped race relations in America for the past 60 years. Issued on the 50th anniversary of the March on Selma (1965), this book is a good companion for anyone who wants to gain insight into the Civil Rights movement, race relations and racism itself.

Author: The Prophet of Life **ISBN**: 978-1-936462-09-4 **ASIN:** B00S05QSXA

Romance Lives

A Collections of romantic love poems. It is divided into three sections. The Hunger about the need for love we all have, the romance about courtship ritual of romancing it takes to create a lasting in the one you choose and the deep emotions involved in making love a lasting love.

Author: The Prophet of Life **ISBN**: **ASIN**:

Life in Verse
A collection of poems about life. The poems and song lyrics are about people, their lives, their hopes and dreams. You can find yourself and people you know in many of them. **Author:** The Prophet of Life **ISBN**:   **ASIN:**

The Best Quotes quotation series
Is a series of books filled with quotes attributed to the Prophet of Life whose quotes have been used by charities, corporations, institutions of Medicine and higher learning. The book includes a license to use any of the quotes as long as they are attributed to The Prophet of Life.

The Best Quotes About God   SP
This short book is filled with some of the more popular quotes about God attrib-uted to The Prophet of Life. It is both thought provoking and inspirational. It is filled with dozens of quotes about God that one can read and copy for personal use.

Author: The Prophet of Life **ISBN:** 978-1-936462-20-9
ASIN: B018P0M8OC

The Best Quotes on General Subjects

This short book is filled with some of the more popular
quotes on general subjects attributed to The Prophet of
Life. The book includes quotes on topics such as life, love,
happiness, crime and punishment, wellness and includes
many of the humorous quotes attributed to The Prophet of
Life. You will find the wit and wisdom in its pages thought
provoking and inspirational. It is filled with dozens of
quotes about God that one can read and copy for personal
use.

Author: The Prophet of Life   **ISBN:**   **ASIN:**
B01M58L9LW

The Best Spiritual Quotes

This book is filled with some of the more popular quotes
on Spiritual Subjects attributed to The Prophet of Life.
Included are quotes on faith, mercy, life lessons, humanity
and spirituality. You should find them to be profound,
thought provoking and inspirational. It is filled with many
pages of quotes that one can read and copy for personal
use.

Author: The Prophet of Life **ISBN:**   **ASIN:**

Children Storybook Series
All books are by Dr. Goose who writes in both prose and rhyming verse.
Classic Children's Stories You've Likely Never Heard SP
Help develop your child's creative abilities and develop their imagination by reading them stories from this book that has no illustrations. Whether it's a story about Prince trying to find the answer to a question, a spider talking about a savior, a kingdom in trouble or a child trying to save the world you will find yourself wanting to read these children's stories with international flavor again and again. This first book in the series is for smaller children.
Author: Dr. Goose ISBN: 978-1-936462-40-7 ASIN: More Classic Children's Stories You've Likely Never Heard   SP

This sequel gives you more unknown classics. The book introduces new characters like a little chicken whose life is similar to a person's and a ballad about a hairy man. There is a story about a prince whose refusal causes an international incident. There is even an updated version of classic children's story everyone knows from different character's points of view. This second book in the series helps tweens and juvenile children creative abilities and develop their imagination as stories from this book that has no illustrations either.

Author: Dr. Goose **ISBN: 978-1-936462-41-4 ASIN:**
My First Book of Stupid Little Fables
Whether the greed of mooches and lunch thieves, sadistic children, or bizarre stories about pets this first installment in the series of irreverently humorous stories with twisted endings about the selfish and the greedy delivers. It even has the stupid little drawings! For Juveniles.

Author: Dr. Goose   **ISBN:** 978-1-936462-44-5 **ASIN:**
My Second Book of Stupid Little Fables
Whether it's well-meaning but incompetent grandmas, egotistical women, sadistic children, or crazy people in shopping centers, this second installment in the series of irreverently humorous stories with twisted endings about the selfish and the greedy delivers. It even has the drawings you love to make fun of just like the first one! For Juveniles. **Author:** Dr. Goose   **ISBN:**   **ASIN:**

Coming Soon E Workbooks and an E Textbook!

A series of mini and one comprehensive E Textbook Under the title of Mr. Wilkins Teaches English by Mark Wilkins

The specific mini textbooks will be on topics such as Reading and Responding to Literature, and Methods for Writing Paragraphs and Essays. The Comprehensive text will include a weekly spelling component and both the mini texts and comprehensive Text will include creative lessons that promote creativity and critical thinking in students while fitting into common core standards. The mini texts will be no more than 99 cents each and the comprehensive text will be under $10!

All of the books are freshly created and contain exclusive intellectual property you won't find in any other texts. These books are perfect for students learning high school English levels 9 & 10 whether you are a classroom teacher or are home schooling your child. We are making the commitment to keep all of the books at low prices to allow parents and school districts to afford texts in the face of shrinking educational budgets. Purchasers will be given an opportunity to receive an email with a printable version of the exercises and assignments as well as links to online testing free of charge.
Author: Mark Wilkins   **ISBN:**   **ASIN:**

Compelling Stories for Adaptation to Short Film
For Film Students
Compelling stories in a set location with six or less characters. Easily adaptable to screenplay with notes on adapting them.
Author: Mark Wilkins   **ISBN:**   **ASIN:**